ISBN 978-0-484-58363-3
PIBN 10804407

This book is a reproduction of an important historical work. Forgotten Books uses
state-of-the-art technology to digitally reconstruct the work, preserving the original format
whilst repairing imperfections present in the aged copy. In rare cases, an imperfection in
the original, such as a blemish or missing page, may be replicated in our edition. We do,
however, repair the vast majority of imperfections successfully; any imperfections that
remain are intentionally left to preserve the state of such historical works.

# THE

# ᴀɪʀ CONCUBINE:

## ᴏʀ, ᴛʜᴇ

# Secret HISTORY

### Of the Bᴇᴀᴜᴛɪꜰᴜʟ

# *ᴀ N E L L ᴀ.*

### Cᴏɴᴛᴀɪɴɪɴɢ,

er Amours with *Albimarides*, P. *Alexis*, &c.
Her Departure from the Court. The Particulars of her Settlement. An Account of several
curious Incidents that happened in the Course
of her Rivalship with Miss *Mordantia*. Faithful Copies of several of her Letters, particularly
one. to ᴘP. *Alexis* on her first finding herself
Pregnant; and another to the Q ——— con-
cerning her Condition ; together with all
other remarkable Occurences thro' the whole
Course of her Intrigues.

*To which is annexed,*

he Lady's Laſt Shift ; or, a Cure
for Shame. A TALE.

---

Dedicated to Five Honourable Maids.

---

---

*L O N D O N.*
Printed for W. Jᴀᴍᴇꜱ, without *Temple-Bar.*
M, DCC, XXXII.
( Price One Shilling.)

## T O

# Five Hon. MAIDS.

*LADIES,*

T your Feet I lay the
following Treatise, and
humbly implore you to
take it under your Care
and Protection, for Rea-
sons which you may ve-
ry well guess, and there is no Necessity
for mentioning them. The Story, tho'
brought from another Country, is lite-
rally true, and is pretty near upon a
Parallel with a certain young Lady,

B         whom

whom Love and Beauty has rendered odious to Virtue; and therefore, as Tenderneſs and Compaſſion. glow in your Breaſts, ſo I hope you will pity the poor *Vanella*, that fallen Angel, who ſacrificed her Fame and Reputation to *Cupid*, and ſhipwrecked her Virtue in his Cauſe.

WHAT an imprudent Part has ſhe played? Could ſhe not *dance without paying the Piper?* But in good truth, ſhe *jigg'd* it about to ſome Tune. You very well know, Ladies, that if every Body's Faults, were printed in their Foreheads, Vizors would be more in Faſhion than Hoop Petticoats; and tho' you might wink at *Vanella's* Frailty, yet I am perſuaded you will cenſure her Conduct in not guarding herſelf againſt a Diſcovery. Lud! Lud! I warrant you that the poor Girl was hugely afraid of *leading Apes in Hell*; but as well to avoid that curſed Fate, as likewiſe dreading the Thoughts of loſing her *Teeming Time*, ſhe reſolved not to live an *Od Maid* in this World, and therefore ventured, like a *Virago*, to be made a *Woman*; and ſo prevent the Odium and Diſgrace which her own Sex would

would caſt upon her, and the malicious
Treatment of our's.

I AM ready to acknowledge, that
*Vanella's* Indiſcretion was great: But
then conſider, fair Ladies, that your
Sex is naturally weak. The *Falling
Sickneſs*, you know, is an hereditary
Diſtemper in moſt Families; it was the
firſt Diſeaſe that crept into the World,
and Mother *Eve* was the firſt Perſon
whom it ſeized. If therefore our Law-
yers will allow Cuſtom and Preſcription
to be good Pleas, *Vanella* ſurely might
plead beſt in her Juſtification. Ye Honourable Maids are alſo ſenſible when
Temptation is ſtrong, Deſire inflamed,
Youth preſſing, and Opportunity in-
viting, 'tis no eaſy Matter to reſiſt the
CRITICAL MINUTE, eſpeci-
ally when Virtue, which ſhould have
guarded, has deſerted Love's *Portal,*
and left it open for the Beſieger to *En-
ter* whenever he is inclined to do it.
Some have capitulated upon honourable
Terms; others, knowing the Generoſi-
ty of the Enemy, have ſurrendered at
Diſcretion; and a generous Foe has often proved kinder to the former than to
the latter.

YOU

YOU will fay, perhaps, that the *Fair Concubine* ought to have been more prudent than to let the Burlinefs about her Hips, and the Shortnefs of her Petticoats difclofed what fhe had been *doing* But I appeal to all the *knowing* Part of your Sex; I appeal even to yourfelves, whether you believe it poffible to abftain from returning *Love for Love* in the CRITICAL MINUTE? For then the Senfes are in a Rapture, and the Thoughts of what may be the Confequence of the amorous Encounter are fwallowed up and loft in the Extafy of Love Enjoyments. There is no Room for *Forecaft* at fuch a Juncture, and the Mind is fo clofely employed about the *Time prefent*, that the future cannot be confulted; but fuppofing that Lovers fhould be fo prudent as to gratify one another by Turns, ye will allow, furely, that a Moiety of the *Fruition* is wanting, and that it is but an *Half Pleafure* at beft. Can ye not tell by Experience that there is Harmony in a *Concert*, and that it ravifhes the Senfes, which a fingle Perfon, tho' his Inftrument be never fo good, cannot effect?

IF

IF any of you have done the *Paw Thing*, you muſt needs own what I have juſt now aſſerted to be true, and impute it not to Diſcretion or prudent Management that ye have eſcaped the publick Shame which befel *Vanella*; for ſome Women, like ſome Fields, are barren through Frigidity, but when that Cauſe is removed, by uſing proper Methods, they will ſoon grow prolific, and very probably produce Fruit *meet for Repentance*.

*VANELLA* was not the firſt, nor will ſhe be the laſt, young Creature that has given a Looſe to Love : Court Ladies, who have had a larger Share of Underſtanding, and more advanced in Years, which ſhould have taught them Wiſdom, have been ſeduced, and I need not go out of this Kingdom for Examples.

WE have an *Engliſh* Proverb which ſays, *There is no harm done when a good Child is got.* If this holds true, then the Memory of *Vanella* will ſmell as ſweet as a Violet. And let me aſſure you, that a Woman, born of noble
Pa-

Parentage, and debauched, even by a Perfon of Quality, if fhe has Wealth at command, values not what malicious Tongues fay of her.

CONSIDER, Ladies, that *Virtue* and *Chaftity* are the brighteft Jewels that can adorn a Woman; their Value is ineftimable, their Lofs irretrievable: Confider therefore, and confider feri-oufly, in what great Eftimation you ought to have them. But if, after all the Advice and Admonition that has been given you, if ye prove deaf to fage and good Counfel, if ye will turn Re-trograde, and follow *Vanella*'s Example, yet buoy not your felves up with the vain Expectation of having as good Provifion for ye, as fhe has. Settle-ments are precarious Things, and it will be too late to infift upon, or demand honourable Terms, when ye are in the Hands of the Enemy; you muft rely then upon his Munificence, and be fub-ject to his Will and Pleafure when he has you in his Power. If therefore ye are determined to difpofe of your pre-cious Jewels, befure to oblige the Pur-chafer to pay ready Money, or at leaft to give ye good Security; if ye act o-

therwife,

therwise, then to your irretrievable
Loss, will be added Folly and Indiscre-
tion, ye will give the World just Cause
to laugh at your Imprudence, and con-
demn your Simplicity.

*I am,*

*With profound Respect,*

*L A D I E S,*

*Your most faithful Counsellor,*

*Your most humble and*

*Most obedient Servant,*

The AUTHOR.

To

# To the READER.

AS no Care or Pains have been spared in collecting Materials from the best and most approv'd Authors for furnishing the following Account of Vanella's Life; and as I have not wilfully omitted any one Point or Circumstance that is of any Moment to her Story, so likewise there is nothing here inserted but what was found in the Records of Time. If the Histories from whence I have taken these Collections are spurious or defective, the Charge ought to be laid at the Doors of their Authors; but there seems to be so much Veracity in them, that no one I believe will make a doubt of their being genuine.

C                    BEAUT

BEAUTY *may very well be compar'd
to Riches, neither of them is pernicious in
itself, but the general Consequence of both
are Presumption, Pride, Arrogancy, Con-
cupisence, wicked Pleasures, and unsati-
able Desire of encreasing that Portion
which People have in Possession. The
Truth of this Assertion is confirm'd by dai-
ly Experience, and I may say, that
Beauty in a Woman, if not accompanied
with a more than ordinary Share of Virtue,
for the most Part terminates in her Ruin;
for though she may indulge her Fancy with
the Thoughts of captivating and securing
the Heart of the Man she loves, yet it
too frequently happens that Beauty renders
a Woman miserable and contemptible: For,
as the* Poet *sings,*

BEAUTY's a gaudy Sign, no more
To tempt the Gazer to the Door;
Within the Entertainment lies,
Far off remov'd from vulgar Eyes.

And

*And when a Man has poſſeſſed her, he values her Beauty no more than as it con-duces to encreaſe his Luſt, and give a dou-ble Reliſh to Fruition. This was the Caſe of* Vanella, *who, if ſhe had preſerved her Chaſtity, might have enjoy'd all the Felicity that this World could afford; but ſhe who was an* Angel of Light *is now become an* Angel of Darkneſs, *and the Stain of her Reputation is indelible. Thus we ſee that Beauty is rather a Curſe than Bleſſing, and how mortifying muſt it be to a beautiful Woman, when ſhe finds herſelf forſaken, even though ſhe has Youth on her Side, and beholds her Lover raveling and wantoning in the Embraces of another, who is older, and not near ſo handſome as ſhe.*

*The Reader will find many Tranſ-actions in this Hiſtory, which have been kept ſecret by Art and Induſtry; and though he muſt needs applaud the Gene-roſity of Prince* Alexis, *yet he cannot in Juſtice vindicate or countenance his Be-*

*baviour*

baviour to Vanella, whose Fame is so much tarnished, that it can never be brought to it's former Lustre. Her History contains many uncommon and surprising Adventures, but as she abused the good Nature and Indulgence of her Royal Mistress, her Fall and Disgrace, has rendered her less pittyed.

Having stript her of her Græcian Habit, I here present her to you in an English Dress; not pompous and gaudy, nor yet abject; but in such Apparel as may not create a Disgust in those who are nice and curious, nor cloy and surfeit them who keep a just Medium between real Love and Luxuriousness: and I heartily wish that Vanella's Misconduct may be a sufficent Caution to other young Ladies not to fall into the same Snare.

THE

# THE
# FAIR CONCUBINE.

THO' *History* and *Biography* may appear to be Twin-Sisters in the Eyes of some People, yet their Affinity, if there is any between them, is remov'd to a far greater Distance than they are aware on; for Historians treats of Things and Times in general, and seldom descends to Particulars; but Biographers are oblig'd to recite the most minute Transactions of the Persons whose Lives he writes, if it be of any Women, or may be conducive to illustrate the Work which he undertakes. I take it for granted, that *Vanella* will be miserably *maul'd* by the *Coquets* of this Age, and undergo the *Lash* of the *Prudes*, from whose Hands no *Quarters* can be expected, though (notwithstanding their formal Pretensions

tensions to Sanctity and Devotion) they are guilty of the like Crime, and reiterate it, as often as they have an Opportunity of doing it.

THE World Expects an Account of every Person who is become notorious for good or bad Actions, and as the Generality of Mankind is for reading the *vicious* rather than the virtuous Part of a Woman's Life, I thought it may not be improper at this Time to gratify their Inclination by introducing *Vanella* upon the stage, and present her to them in her natural Colours.

*AGIS*, King of *Lacedemonia*, was a magnanimous and virtuous Monarch; he married *Elóifa*, the Daughter of a *Græcian* Prince, and their Nuptial Bed was grac'd with a numerous Issue. *Alexis*, his eldest Son, was educated in sound Learning and moral Principles, and being Heir Apparent to his Father's Kingdom, had, when he arrived at the Years of Maturity, an Apartment allotted to him, and an Appendage sufficient to support the Grandeur and Dignity of his Birth.

QUEEN *Elóifa* was a Lady of strict Piety and Virtue, and took into her Train six young Ladies, among whom *Vanella* was one, and the Queen had a more than common

mon

mon Regard and Compaſſion for her, on account of an unhappy Indiſpoſition which
her Father, a *Græcian* Lord, labour'd
under. She was young and beautiful, had
a competant Share of Wit and good Senſe,
but took too much Freedom in her Conver-
ſation, which becoming habitual, proved to
be the Deſtruction of her Character and Reputation. Her Levity was conſpicious to
every one, and it had taken ſuch deep Root,
that neither Example nor Precept could era-
dicate it; therefore to prevent, if poſſible,
the fatal Conſequence which was appre-
hended might enſue, it was judged proper
to provide a Husband for her, and a
Match was propoſed between her and *Leonides*, who was a *Lacedemonian* Lord, and
had been a Commander in the Army. But
it fortunately happen'd for him, that before
the Treaty of Marriage was concluded, he
was ſent Ambaſſador by his Royal Maſter
to adjuſt the Difference that aroſe between
two Neighbouring Potentates; and there we
ſhall leave him and return to *Vanella*.

SOME Hiſtorians, whom I have con-
ſulted for the more regular Formation of this
Hiſtory, ſeem to queſtion the Veracity of
what their Predeceſſors have alleged in Vin-
dication of every particular Expreſſion and
Paſſage contain'd in the following Para-
graphs, but allow the whole in general to
be

be genuine; I have therefore chofe to infert them, fince they do not carry a Face of Impartiality, and leave to the Reader to form Judgment of them as he fhall think proper.

THIS young Lady had a Multitude of Admirers, and among the reft who made their Addreffes to her, *Albimarides*, a young Nobleman belonging to King *Agis*, had the firft Place in her Affection. His Levity was upon a Level with hers, which principally recommended him to her good Graces; fhe efteem'd herfelf to be the happieft Perfon upon Earth while fhe was in his Company, and thought he could not be too frequent in the Repitition of his Vifits, tho' he was at the fame time paving a Way for her Ruin. Love was the Topick by which he infinuated himfelf into her Favour, but alas! *honourable Love* was a Stranger to his Heart; for he ufed it as a Cloak to cover his libidinous Defigns. They grew fo very familiar, that fhe indulg'd him in all the Liberties he was pleafed to take, one only excepted, and it is poffible fhe would not have denied him *That*, had he *pufhed hard* for it; but in a fmall fpace of Time he accomplifhed it with much Facility.

COMING one Evening to her Apartment, he furprifed her as fhe fat mufing in

her

her Bed-Chamber, but when the Fit was over, they renewed their Custom of toying together; and leaning his Head on her Bosome, she puting one Hand about his Neck, and stroking his Face with the other, he took a Paper out of his Pocket, on which the following Lines were written, which he sung to her.

*WHAT is* Beauty, *but a Gin*
*To ensnare and trap Folks in ?*
Cupid's *Net to catch a Heart,*
*Natures Picture without* Art *;*
*With the* Lilly *joins the* Rose,
*Stornger Charms their Union shews ;*
*Now they bloom, and now are gay*
*Like the wanton Month of* May :
*But when Age begin t'appear,*
*And the Autumn does draw near,*
Beauty *sickens at the Sight,*
*Then she dreads approaching Night ;*
*Wan and languid are her Eyes,*
*Weak her Power did surprise,*
*All her boasted Charms decay,*
Rose *and* Lilly *fade away.*

*ALBIMARIDES* sung the Words with so much Humour that *Vanella* resolved to have them though she paid ever so dear for the Purchase; and he perceiving that her Resolution was unalterable, determined to have a valuable Consideration for them.

D                                       To

To this End he artfully kept her in suspence
for some time, now seeming to gratify her
Desire, and then again to put her off with
feigned Excuses, all which tended only to
make her more eager to obtain them. *Hark,
you, my Lord,* says she, patting him on the
Face, and alluring him with her Blushes,
*give me the Song, and we will take the 'Plea-
sure of looking Babies in one another's Eyes.*
*Faith, Madam,* answered *Albimarides* with
a smiling Countenance, *there is a great deal
more Pleasure to be found in getting of Babies.*
*It may be so truly,* reply'd *Vanella* very demure-
ly, *but let us leave this idle Talk, and give me
the Song, for I will have it do what you can.*
Thereupon she snatched the Paper out of his
Hand, and put it into her Bosom. *Nay,*
says *Albimarides, if you will take it by Force,
you shall take something else in the like Manner.* He then took her in his Arms, and
having almost smothered her with Kisses,
laid her upon the Bed, and she finding him
preparing the Way for Enjoyment, said,
*O Lud! O Lud! What are you doing?* My
Maid's in the next Room, and will hear us;
O fy, fy, my Lord, pray now forbear, you
will ruin me,——Oh! Oh! I shall be un-
done for ever,——I swear I will cry out,——
Oh! Oh! ———Whether the Extasy was
so great she could not cry out, or whether he
prevented her, by reiterated Kisses, I will
not take upon me to determine, it is certain
that

that she soon grew as tame, and lay as quiet as a Wife.

HISTORY informs us that his Lordship *crack'd the Shell*, but makes no mention of his having *found* the *Kernel*, so that we are left in the dark in Relation to that particular Point; we are likewise left to ourselves to guess how often he rallied and repeated the *Onset* before he retreated out of the Field.

*VANELLA* perceiving the Hour to draw nigh when she must appear at Court, was oblig'd to change her Headcloaths, which was very much rumpled by *Albimarides*; and when he appeared among the Ladies, any body who had been so curious, might have perceived that the young Lord and she had been doing what was not justifiable, for her guilty Conscience flew in her Face when he came near her, and discovered it self with frequent Blushes. However, she got the upperhand of it at last, and carried herself in the best Manner she was capable of doing; and though she trembled at the Thoughts of his speaking to her, yet she greatly desired it; but she was very much vex'd when she saw him converse and take a more than ordinary Liberty (as she imagined) with the other young Ladies. Not able to curb her Jealousy, she approach'd

D                    and

and made one among them, then with a kind of haughty and difdainful Air, faid, *Ladies take care how you converfe with the Lord* Albimarides, *he has a foft, bewitching Tongue fufficient to delude a* Veftal *Virgin. You fpeak very* feelingly, *Madam,* fays one of the Ladies, whofe Name was *Medofaria, and we hope he has* not deluded *you; but we thank you for your good Advice, and in my Opinion no-body is fo capable of fhewing where the dangerous Rock lies, as the Perfon who has been* Shipwreck'd *upon it. Truly,* replied *Vanella,* with all the Arrogance imaginable, *I did not direct my Difcourfe to you,* Medofaria ; *but fince you have taken a Freedom that does not become you, I muft tell you plainly, that no Man will venture a Shipwreck with you, or even to go on board your Veffel, which fails fo very aukwardly, and is fo wretchedly built, that fhe will not anfwer the Helm.*

HOW far they would have carried their Refentment, had they not been interrupted by the Queen *Eloifa,* who was going to take the Air, and on whom they were obliged to attend, no body can tell ; however their Difcourfe having been buz'd about the Court, foon reached the Queen's Ear, who reprimanded the two Antagonifts in a very kind and maternal Manner; and as fhe was all Goodnefs in her felf, fhe took all the

Care

Care imaginable to breed up the young Ladies in virtuous Principles, and to prevent any Jealousy that might arise among them on Account of who had the greatest Share in her Favour, for she treated each of them alike. This is an Example, which, as it is wanted in most Families, 'tis hoped will be followed by every one.

WHETHER the Queen suspected that *Vanella* had play'd a *Slippery Trick*, or that her Beauty might entice some of the Courtiers to make unlawful Addresses to her, and be the Occasion of her Ruin, is hard to determine; but certain it is that she sent for *Vanella* privately, and among many other Questions which she put to her, demanded to know if the Lord *Albimarides* had a mind to seduce her to a Violation of her Chastity? *Vanella* was so surprised at this unexpected Question, that she could not readily give an Answer; but as soon as she recovered herself from the Confusion she was in, she said, *Madame*, as your Majesty has done me the Honour to admit me into your Family, and have used me with the Tenderness and Affection of a *Mother, my Duty obliges me to give you all the Satisfaction that I am capable of in this particular; I beg leave therefore to declare to your Majesty, that the young Lord* Albimarides *never offer'd any thing that was rude or dishonourable.*

The

The Queen, not doubting the Veracity of what she said, seem'd to be well satisfied, and told her by the by, that she could not with Honour retract from the Match with *Leonides*, which was in effect as good as concluded. To this *Vanella* answered, *Madam, I have a great Value and Respect for* Leonides, *but as I always shewed an Aversion to that Match, except only a seeming Compliance, which filial Duty extorted from me, I hope I shall be held excusable if I refuse to make us both miserable, which would be the certain Consequence of such a Marriage; in my humble Opinion there is too great a Disparity in our Ages, which is the only Objection I raise, believing that Lord* Leonides *would be a very good Husband, and make any other Woman happy.*

THE Queen did not urge this Affair any farther, but dismiss'd *Vanella*, having caution'd her in the most friendly Manner, not to make a false Step, or do any Thing that might bring a Blemish on her Reputation.

AS soon as *Vanella* came to her Apartment, she sent for *Albimarides*, to whom she related all that had pass'd between the Queen and her, and told him she did not question but her Majesty would talk to him about it, and therefore thought proper to forewarn him, that he might be prepar'd

with

with an Anſwer, if the Queen ſhould ask him any Queſtion. *Albimarides* approv'd her Conduct; and taking her in his Arms, repeated Kiſſes prevented her from uttering one Word; then uſing a Familiarity not proper to be related, ſhe diſengaging her Lips from his, ſaid, *What, my Lord, will you not give over 'till you have ruined me for ever? but I fear you have already done it, and how can I reſiſt the Man who has diſarm'd my Heart?* The Reader may gueſs the Conſequence; for as the Poet very pathetically expreſſes it,

*What followed next was paſt the Power of
   Verſe,*
*Beyond the reach of Fancy to rehearſe.*

WOMEN have naturally a Tenderneſs and Affection for the Perſon who ſpoils them of their Virginity, and there is nothing more common than when they have gratified the Inclinations of the Man they love, to permit him to reiterate them as frequently as he deſires, eſpecially if he has exercifed himſelf ſtrenuouſly. This we ſee verified in *Vanella*, who was no leſs than a Slave to the Libidinous Deſires of *Albimarides*.

IN a little time this young Lady's Countenance began to grow pale and wan; and her fainting Fits at Court, which appear'd the more vifible, as fhe took the greater Pains to conceal them, together with feveral other Symtoms, occafion'd it to be whifper'd about that fhe was Pregnant. This News was fweeter than *Nectar* and *Ambrofia* to the two young Ladies, *Medofaria* and *Mordantia*, who were her Rival Companions, and envied her on account of her Beauty, feared that one Day or other fhe might engrofs the Favours of *Alexis*, as fhe had already fecur'd thofe of *Albimarides*: And truly it muft be confefs'd that *Vanella*'s bright Charms would have melted the frozen Heart of an Hermit, and obliged him to facrifice at her *Shrine*, nay to have offered a whole *Hecatomb* at her *Alter*, had he been fo well provided.

*VANELLA* feeing fhe was nearer the Time of her Delivery than fhe imagined, kept her Bed one Day to confider what Method fhe fhould take to conceal her big Belly ; and as fhe had confin'd her felf to her Apartment, it gave Birth to various Speculations. Queen *Eloifa* having been informed that the young Lady was very much indifpofed, ordered her own Phyficians to attend her, and make their Report next Day, which they failed not to do, and gave it as their Opinions that the Country Air would very much conduce to the Recovery of her

Health

Health; and thereupon she sent one of her Ladies to charge *Vanella* in her Name not to get out of Bed 'till her Majesty came, which would be in the Evening.

THIS you must needs think was a great Surprise to *Vanella*; but it is impossible to comprehend the Confusion she was in, when she saw Queen *Eloisa* approached her Bed-Side, who commanded her to relate the Cause of her Grief without any Disguise or Subtlety. *Madam*, said the trembling *Fair One*, if I had taken Warning by the *Moth* which plays about the Candle till it has burn'd its Wings, I should not have been in this Condition; but I have play'd the Fool with a certain Lord too long, and now he slights and contemns me, and does all that lies in his Power to make me become the Jest of *Medofaria* and *Merdantia*. I heartily wish, answered the good and sage Queen, that you have not been *playing something* else with him; I am loth to give Credit to what is confidently reported; but if you have been so imprudent as to make a false Step, I advise you to repent of your Error. In the mean Time I lay an Injuction upon you not to receive a Visit from him, or converse with him, either personaly, by Message, Writing, or otherwise, without my Approbation. She then was graciously pleafed to give her the best Counsel, with Di-

rections

rections for her future Behaviour; adding, that the Phificians judg'd it proper that she should go into the Country, and if she thought she could bear the Fatigue of a Journey, the sooner she began it, the greater Benefit she would receive by it.

AS soon as *Vanella* could equip herself with such Necessaries as she might want, she arose very early one Morning, and walking about a Mile from the Palace of *Lacedæmonia*, found a Chariot waiting for her, and several Servants well mounted and arm'd, who escorted her to a Sea-port Town about 30 Leagues distance from thence.

HERE she led a kind of recluse Life, seldom going abroad but for the Benefit of the Air; but complaining one Evening of a violent Pain in her Back, she had the good Fortune to have it *in her Arms* before the Morning.

AS soon as she recovered her Strength and Complection, she went to a City about ten Miles from the Place where she had *laid in*; but what became of the Babe, or whether it was Male or Female I cannot take upon me to ascertain, History being deficient therein. Here was a vast Concourse of Nobility and Gentry, and *Vanella* appeared every Day in Publick, and resorted ſo all their Plays, Sports, and Paſtimes, on purpoſe to be taken notice of, for ſhe hop'd thereby to obviate the Malice of her Enemies. Perceiving moſt of the Company to withdraw from thence, this young Lady likewiſe ſet out for *Lacedemonia*, and, upon her Arrival at Court, met with a generous Reception ; even her two inveterate Rivals *Medoſ ria* and *Mordantia*, with unparallel'd Hypocracy, congratulated her upon her Return, and the Recovery of her Health. But their Cob-web Net was too thin not to be diſcover'd, and too weak to hold *Vanella* ; however, aſſuming a careleſs Air, ſhe thanked them for their Civility, then turning ſhort, and looking upon them with Diſdain, ſhe joined in Company with the Court Ladies.

SHE now ſhines with double Luſtre to what ſhe had done before, and was more beautiful (if poſſible) than the celebrated *Helen*. She was inform'd one Day that Prince *Alexis* deſign'd to make her his Miſtreſs ; this pleaſed her exceedingly, and ſhe determined not to be too eaſy in giving her Conſent, leſt it might pall his Inclination, and give him Occaſion to have the leſs Value and Reſpect for her: nor yet dally with him too long for fear he might forſake her, and take to another, but obſerve a due Decorum and Medium between the two Extreams,

KING

KING *Agis* went to *Rusticate*, at a small
Seat which he had purchased, delightfully
situated on a large and pleasant River. He
took his Queen and Family with him, with
necessary Attendants; and riding abroad
one Day to take the Diversion of killing
some Game in one of his Parks, and being
very intent upon the Pursuit of his Sport,
Prince *Alexis* soon prevail'd with *Vanella* to
retire with him to a Covert; here he dis-
mounted, and fastening his Horse to a Tree,
as he had also done the young Lady's, he
took her from her Saddle, and led her to a
Bank of Dazies, in the Midst of a pleasant
Grove, where they sat secure from the
scorching Beams of the Sun.

HERE they spent several Hours to their
mutual Satisfaction, in kissing, toying, and
Love Embraces; insomuch, that the Evening was pretty far spent, before they were
aware of it. This filled them with some
perplexing Thoughts, but making a Virtue
of Necessity, the Prince plac'd *Vanella*
on her Horse, and mounting his own, they
rode directly to the Park-gate, which, to
their great Surpise, was lock'd, and no body attended to open it. The Prince calling
to Mind that there was a House at a small
Distance, which had a Passage into the Road,
galloped thither with his Mistress, and both
alighting

aligting, they knock'd at the Door. No
body was at home but a Servant, who looking out of the Window, and seeing Prince
*Alexis*, and a Gentlewoman with him, hasten-
ed to let them in. He put up their Horses,
and ask'd if they would please to drink a
Glass of Wine, for he could furnish them with
as good as any in *Greece*. To this they con-
sented, and went up Stairs into a Room,
where they continued till the Evening grew
dusky ; then, according to what had
been agreed on between them, *Vanella* took
a By Road which led her to the Seat of
King *Agis*; and then the Prince ask'd the
Servant if he knew who he was ? the Fellow
answered, *It is not my Business, Sir, to know
any Gentleman, who is not willing to be
known.* *Alexis* was very well pleased with
this Answer, and rewarding the Fellow
went to his own Country-house, and soon
after he came home, proper Servants were
sent for the Horses.

WHEN *Vanella* came to her Apartment,
she made what haste she could to dress her
self in order to appear before her Royal
Mistress ; but *Medosaria* and *Mordantia* being sworn Enemies to this young Lady, and
having vowed to work her Overthrow (tho'
all their Schems were of no other Effect
than to promote the Interest of *Vanella*)
went privately, under a Pretence of a Visit,
hoping

hoping, however, not to find her within, and then would have had a plausible Reason to say that she had been with the Prince, for they were missed much about the same Time. They also dispatch'd a Messenger to the House of *Alexis*, but were miserably baulked in their Expectations : For they found *Vanella* sitting on a Couch, with a Book in her Hand, and Word was brought them that the Prince was at Dinner. They were extreamly vex'd at these Disappointments, for though they had substantial Ground for Suspicion, they could not by all their Stratagems make a Discovery; yet *Mordantia*, filled with Rage and Envy, very pertly said, *Madam, What is become of the Prince?* *Vanella* replied, *When I am made Keeper of the Prince, I shall then be able to answer such an Impertinent Question; but I suppose, Madam, you are very well satisfied that Prince* Alexis *is now at Dinner.* This was a Mortification to *Mordantia*, who concluded that *Vanella* had overheard what the Messenger had told her; and resolving, if possible, to irritate her to the highest Degree, said, *Allow that you are not the Prince's Keeper, but I suppose you would willingly be kept by him. If that should ever come to pass,* replied *Vanella, I do assure you I shall not be jealous of YOU; for I believe Prince* Alexis *has a better Taste than to change a* Peach *for a* Quince. *Truly,* Mordantia, *all your Arti-*

*fices*

*fices will not avail you; I can see through them, and must tell you, that you were not cut out for a* Petticoat Plotter.

MORDANTIA, imagining that *Vanella's* Words glanc'd strong at her, though they seem'd to be pointed at *Medosaria,* arose from her Chair, and with Indignation in her Countenance, said, *I think it is very proper that we take leave of the Lady, otherwise she may grow Angry, and then how will she be able to entertain the* Prince, *from whom I suppose she expects a Visit after Dinner?* To this *Vanella* answered, *If* Prince Alexis *will do me so much Honour, my* Duty *obliges me, even though Inclination were wanting, to give him* the civilest Reception ; *but,* Ladies, *as such a Sight would put you into the most bitter Agonies, I advise you to retire in Time.* Envy *is a corroding Cancer in the Mind, and furrows many a handsome Face even before the Autumn of Life draws near ; not that I think it can do any prejudice to* you, Mordantia, *you may still proceed in following the Example of the* Viper *in the Fable, and gnaw the File till you break every Tooth in your Head.* But *that ye both may have something to Employ your Thoughts for a while, I desire you to remember, that* Venus *carried off the golden* Prize, *and that* Paris, *who gave it her as a Reward which her Beauty justly claimed, was the* Son of a King : *But mistake me not, for there*

*there is no Room to infer from hence, that I think either of ye a Juno, or a Pallas, though you may call the former your Patroness, who, if Fame may be credited, founded the School wherein poor Mortals learn* Billingsgate Re-torick.

THE Season of the Year advancing which invited the Nobility and Gentry to breath the Country Air, King *Agis* removed with all his Court to one of his Palaces, situated at some Distance from *Lacedemonia.* Prince *Alexis*, having a strong Desire to make an Experiment of *Vanella's* Sincerity, thought that the best Method he could take, was to give her Cause to be jealous; to effect this he talk'd very freely with *Medosaria* and *Mordantia*, and to the latter, when in Company one Evening with *Vanella*, he made a Present of a *Gold Box*, inlaid with the richest Jewels: Nay, History tell us, that he proceeded to a farther Length, he attempted a Peasant's Wife to his Embraces, who being obstinate in her Refusal, and he earnestly insisting on a Compliance, she at last called out, and alarm'd her Husband, who came immediately to her Relief. They either did not, or would not know who he was; and therefore handled him in a very rough Manner, which soon reach'd the Ears of *Vanella.* She now became extreamly

jealous

jealous, and not able to retain her Mind any longer, wrote him a Letter to the following purpose.

*My dear Prince,*

"KINDLY receive this Letter, which comes from her whose Soul you have set on Fire, and who wishes to live no longer than she proves constant to you. Happy, thrice happy I was when in my Arms you panting lay, and spoke a thousand pretty Things to me. Our mutual Love produc'd mutual Joys, nor did we think ourselves lavish therein. But now Millions of Furies invade my Breast, ten thousand anxious Doubts disturb my Mind, and Night and Day I can find no Peace. *Rage* and *Jealousy* domineer and play the Tyrant over me by Turns; methinks I am the Laughing-stock of the Court, and when I approach my *Royal Mistress*, my Heart conscious of it's Guilt is struck with a panick Fear, and when I retire, burning with an eternal Flame, I find my Apartment, which was my Paradise when you were there, is now become a Hell. O *Alexis*, the Tortures of a Rack are nothing in Comparison to what I feel; yet these, and more than these, I suffer for your Sake. Tell me, dear Prince, what have I done; what

F "Cause

" Caufe have I given you to forfake me ?
" can *Medofaria* vie with me for Nobility
" of Birth, or *Mordantia* ftand in Competi-
" tion with *Vanella* for Beauty? why then
" am I flighted and they carrefs'd? how
" often have you told me that I had a Mul-
" titude of Charms, and that the *Graces*
" were proud of their Attendance on me ?
" Is it then poffible that you can con-
" defcend to follicite a *Plebean* Matron,
" the Wife of a poor Peafant, to grant you a
" Favour, which *Venus*, if fhe were on Earth,
" would be proud to grant you? I have a
" thoufand Things to fay, but my Spirits
" fleet fo faft, that my trembling Hand can
" only let you know, except I fee you
" quickly, the next News you hear will be
" the untimely Death of the forfaken and
" diftracted,

*VANELLA.*

THE Prince was fenfibly affected with this Letter, which gave him great Uneafi-nefs, and being now convinc'd of *Vanella's* Sincerity, wifhed that he had not put it to the Teft ; but to comfort the young Lady in her Affliction, he fent word by the Perfon who brought the Letter, that he would not fail of complying with what fhe feem'd to defire.

IN

IN the Evening Prince *Alexis* visited *Vanella*, who, as soon as she saw him, arose from her Couch, but her Joy was so great that she fainted, and had certainly fallen on the Ground, if the Prince had not saved her by catching her in his Arms, tho' she soon recovered her Senses, yet it was some time before she could speak to him; he perceiv'd that she endeavoured to do it, but her Words could find no Utterance. The Prince seeing the Condition she was in, caress'd her most affectionately, and us'd the tenderest Expressions imaginable; in the mean while her Eyes were fix'd upon him; she often sighed and groaned, grasped his Hand fast, and at last, strugling hard to declare her Mind, recovered her Speech, and spoke to him after the following Manner.

*O my Prince, I know not which is greatest, the Torments which you created and I suffered, or the Joy I now receive from your Arms. Believe me, my* Alexis, *I was upon the Verge of* Despair, *and should have cast my self into the Bottomless Gulph, had you not prevented me by your verbal Answer to my Letter; and now your Presence enlivens my Hopes, and bids me live. Methinks that I am just awaken'd from a most hedious and frightful Dream, and I am resolutely determined that Nothing, but the like Occasion, shall disturb my future Peace and Tranquility.* To this

the

the Prince replied. *I do assure you,* Vanella, *I will never give you a second Cause to complain, and what I have done was only to try whether you were* Sincere *in your Love and* Friendship *for my* Person, *of which I am now fully convinc'd.* You must needs own, replied Vanella, *that it was a very severe Tryal; but, my dear* Prince, *your kind Promise, and the Assurance you give me that you'r satisfied with my* Sincerity, *have doubly recompenced all my* Sufferings.

PRINCE *Alexis,* to divert *Vallenv,* shifted this melancholly Scene, and making Love the Subject of their Discourse, they spent several Hours in the most *agreeable* Manner, and to the great Joy and Satisfaction of each other. During the Residence of King *Agis* in the Country, they carried on their Intrigues as plausibly as the Nature of the Affair would admit; nor did they desist upon the Return of the Court to *Ladedemonia.*

IN a few Weeks *Vanella* became pregnant, which, as it encreased every Day, she could not conceal from the prying Eyes of *Mordantia* and *Medosaria,* and as she was passing by these two youg Ladies, when they were talking together, the former said to her, *I think,* Vanella, *you grow* fat *and* lean *like the* Rabits, *but with this Difference, that their*

Change

*Change happens in one Month, and yours in nine.* Vanella, without Hesitation, made Answer, *If I do,* Mordantia, *you must acknowledge that I keep my Fat much longer than you did the* Gold-Box ; *and let me tell you, there is one you know, that would number herself among the happiest* Persons *on Earth, if her Condition could suffer a* Change ; *she has try'd to effect it, but the Labour was lost on both Sides, for there are some Creatures in the World who are naturally Barren. For my Part, I freely own, that if* Prince Alexis *had made me a Present of a* Ring, *a* Box, *or a* Watch, *neither Threats or Promises should have prevailed on me to affront him so grossly as to return it after I had kept it a While.*

HEREUPON *Vanella* withdrew, and sending for one who was her Confident, they consulted on what Method they should ake, and at last concluded to retire to a Country Village named *Egaira,* about five Leagues from *Lacedemon:* Soon after her Departure she wrote a Letter to Queen *Eloisa,* in the *Laconic* Style, and to this Purpose;

*Most Gracious Madam,*

" I BEG leave to inform you, that I am
" with Child by Prince *Alexis* ; for
" which Reason I have retired from Court,
" and think it not proper to return till I
have

" have *Laid in,* or some Provision be
" made for me ; which is certainly very
" requisite."

THE Queen was greatly surprised when
she read the Letter, and sending for the
Prince, shewed it to him, and asking whether
the Contents were true, the Prince bow-
ing with profound Reverence and Respect,
answered in the Affirmative ; the good
Queen chequed him for being guilty of such
a Crime, but a Reconciliation was soon
brought about.

*VANELLA,* sending for her Uncle,
revealed every Thing to him, who under-
took to pacify the Lord her Father, and
re-establish her in his Favour ; and when he
had effected this, he hired a House for her
ready furnished in the *Basilican Square,* to
which she returned, and she had as much
Attendance as any Person of her Rank and
Quality could desire.

AS soon as it was rumoured that *Vanella* had taken a House, several of the
Court-Ladies, and others of the greatest
Distinction, came to visit her; some out of
Curiosity, and others who had a Friendship
and Value for her, to condole with her in
the *unhappy* State she was in. But she, not
daunted at what they said, with a magnanimous

nimous Heart told them, she look'd upon her self to be in the *happiest* Condition of any Woman upon Earth, which she would not change with any Subject in *Lacedemonia*; for she had a large Share of the Prince's Favour, and esteem'd it more Honour to be with Child by him, than to be made a Dutchess. *Alexis* came frequently to her House *incognito*, and being now under no Apprehension of an Interruption, they enjoyed each others Company with double Pleasure. When *Vanella* perceived that the Prince was delighted with her big Belly, she smiling said, I hope, that in a short Time I shall be able to send you the joyful News of the Birth of a Duke; to which the Prince answered, Such News, *Vanella*, will be acceptable to me even at Midnight, and especially if it be accompanied with an Information of your being in as good Health, as can be expected from a Person under the like Circumstances with youself. *Vanella* thanked him for his kind and tender Expressions, and said, She would do herself the Honour to take Care he should be punctually obey'd in every thing ; adding, that she requested him, in Case she should die in Child-Bed, to make a handsome Provision for the Infant, whether Male or Female, which he promised should be certainly performed.

THE

THE *Gracian* Hiftorians do further ob-
ferve, that fo great was the Goodnefs, and
fo very wonderful the Condefcenfion of
Queen *Elóifa*, that fhe permitted herfelf to
be prevail'd upon to let *Vanella* attend her
in private one Day after her Departure from
Court, *Vanella* having a ftrong Defire to
pay her Duty and Refpect to her Majefty,
and to fubmit herfelf entirely to her.

BUT now I fhall confider the Hiftorian's
Account of a Settlement faid to be made
by Prince *Alexis* for this *Fair Concubine,*
and that is as follows, *viz.* Forty thoufand
Crowns to purchafe Plate, and furnifh a
Houfe for her; Eight thoufand Crowns *per
Annum* during her Life; and four thoufand
Crowns more *per Annum* during the Pleafure
of the Prince.

AT the Time of this Hiftory being fent
to the Prefs, *Vanella* had about two Months
to go, as fhe *reckon'd* herfelf; that is, fhe
expected to be brought to Bed in the fifth
Month in the Year.

THE Houfe which was taken for *Vanella*
not being fo convenient as was expected,
her Sifter-in-Law, being reconciled to her,
hired another, which thay went about
to furnifh with all Expedition; Plate
**was**

was brought, many Hands were employ'd in making *Child-bed Linnen*, a Nurse was provided, and she wanted nothing that was requisite for a young Lady in her Condition.

THE Vacancy, occasion'd by *Vanella*'s withdrawing from the Court of *Lacedemonia*, was soon fill'd up, and so great was *Mordantia*'s Interest, that she was put in Possession of the Apartment which her Rival had possessed; tho' this was some Comfort to her, yet she had the Mortification to find, that by all her Plots and Contrivances, she could not eject *Vanella* out of Prince *Alexis*'s Favour, and *Worm* herself into it. However, she would not Despair, for she believed that if *Vanella* should die in Childbed, she might rivet herself in the Prince's good Graces: and if she recover'd, then she hoped in due Time to make him Jealous, and by abandoning the beautiful *Vanella*, she might supply her Place.

JEALOUSY is without Doubt a Sort of Plenty in the Mind, and hurries those whom it has seized to unwarrantable Lengths; the Methods they pursue to ruin their Rivals, generally end in their own Destruction, and as it has the greatest Power over the Minds of Women, so its Strength is manifested to be the strongest, when the contending Parties are of a superior Rank and

Station

Station, and the Object of their Defire moves in a Sphere much lighter than their own. They adore and gaze upon the *rifing Sun*, till its Luftre firft dazzles, and afterwards deprives them of their Sight ; The *Eagle* alone can, with Safety, behold its radiant Beams ; *Vanella* was that *Eagle*, fhe could tower aloft, bask in its Bays with Safety, and wanton in its Meridian Glory. But, alas! her ploting Rivals were oblig'd to pore upon their Mother Earth, and receive fuch Comfort from her at Second Hand, as the *enlivening Sun* was pleafed to communicate to them.

# The Lady's laſt Shift; *or a* Cure for Shame.

## *A TALE.*

*V*ENUS of *Love* and *Beauty* Queen,
  Inſpire my Verſe, direct my Pen,
That it may fair *Vanella* ſhew,
Lovely as thee, and Wanton too;
In Pride of Youth, and Beauty gay,
As *July* ripe, as ſweet as *May.*.

*Fortune* favouring ſtill the Fair,
Took young *Vanella* to her Care,
Plac'd *her* amidſt the Joys of State,
Where Pomp and Pleaſure on *her* wait,
And Threw — to make *her* Bliſs compleat,
Even great *Alexis* at *her* Feet.

Who doth not gay *Alexis* know,
By Birth a Lord, by Dreſs a Beau,
So form'd to give Love's fierce Alarms,
That all to him reſign their Charms.

Proud

Proud if their Beauty can fubdue,
Him whom the Nymphs with *Envy* view;
Towards whom each am'rous *Fair-one* turns,
For whom the Courtly Circle burns.
And full as much Complaifance *fhew*.
As if in a *Seraglio*.

But bright *Vanella*, lucky Maid,
To love *Alexis's* Heart betray'd,
For *her* fet out with Care to view,
His powder'd Front, and *fliffen'd Cue*.
The Youth the Darling of the *Fair*,
Defpifing them, had fix'd on *her*,
His Eyes where-e'er *her* Charms they met,
With a peculiar *Stare* were fet,
With languid Looks on *her* they roll,
And fpeak the Paffion of his Soul;
Each Word, each Act, his Love proclaim,
And Sighs half breath'd fan the foft Flame.
At laft——For Silence had been vain,
He told the *Fair one* all his Pain;
How much his Heart was in her Power,
And what from Scorn he fhould endure.
But the *bright Nymph* had ne'er defign'd,
To be to fuch a Youth unkind;
Charm'd with his Title, Pomp and Shew,
Charm'd with the Lord, and with the Beau;
*She* to *Alexis's* Paffion gave,
All that his warmeft Wifh could crave.

The

The *beauteous Creature* thus enjoy'd,
Grew some spiteful Folks, say cloy'd.

But *ill-luck* did at last prevail,
Here comes the *Burthen* of my *Tale*;
*Vanella* now began to swell,
And Love by its Effects tell
At *her* Wits end to him she flies,
There Raves, and Sighs, and Stamps, and
(Cries;

While poor *Alexis* knew not how,
T'appease *her*, or what best to do.
At length the enamour'd *Pair* agreed,
From Town *she* should depart with speed;
And lie *in cog* till *she* had brought,
The smiling *Issue* of *her Fault*;
And then—quoth He--my Love again,
Shall shine the *brightest* of the Train,
My Power shall still protect *thy Fame*,
And Greatness leave no Room for *Shame*.

Ye *Fair Ones* from *her* Fate be Wise,
Since now *detected* all Despize,
That Beauty which before did prove,
The *Butt* of Envy and of Love,
Yet if her Name ye would obtain,
Your Search give o'er —— since it is *Vain*.

*F I N I S.*

CPSIA information can be obtained
at www.ICGtesting.com
Printed in the USA
BVHW04*1355210918
528174BV00011B/542/P